W9-CFF-765

OCT - - 2023

THREE TASKS FOR A DRAGON

For Emma, who wrangled the text,
and for P.J. himself, who flew the dragon
to unimagined heights
EC

For Heather
PJL

This is a work of fiction. Names, characters, places, and incidents are either
products of the author's imagination or, if real, are used fictitiously.

Text copyright © 2023 by Eoin Colfer
Illustrations copyright © 2023 by P.J. Lynch

All rights reserved. No part of this book may be reproduced, transmitted, or stored in an information
retrieval system in any form or by any means, graphic, electronic, or mechanical, including
photocopying, taping, and recording, without prior written permission from the publisher.

First US edition 2023

Library of Congress Catalog Card Number 2022923385
ISBN 978-1-5362-2999-8

23 24 25 26 27 28 APS 10 9 8 7 6 5 4 3 2 1

Printed in Humen, Dongguan, China

This book was typeset in Centaur.
The illustrations were done in pencil and colored digitally.

Candlewick Press
99 Dover Street
Somerville, Massachusetts 02144

www.candlewick.com

Three Tasks for a Dragon

EOIN COLFER

ILLUSTRATED BY P.J. LYNCH

CANDLEWICK PRESS

CHAPTER ONE

The Disappointing Prince

ONCE THERE WAS A PRINCE IN THE KINGDOM OF LAGIN WHO WAS such a disappointment to his royal stepmother that she sought to have him banished from the realm.

"You cannot ride a horse, Prince Lir," said Queen Nimh one evening after dinner in the great hall. "You can barely lift a sword. And you cannot summon the wolfhounds."

The last accusation was peculiar because until this very day, and for the past five hundred years, the act of summoning the wolfhounds had been little more than a story passed down by campfire bards.

Summoning the wolfhounds involved standing on the balcony built into the Wolfhound's Tooth, a towering spire of sandstone and ivory, and hoping the large shaggy dogs gathered below.

The legend had it that in times gone by, kings had been chosen because of their magical bond with the majestic wolfhounds of Lagin city and dominion, but no true wolfhound king had summoned the hounds in half a millennium—and for coronations and royal weddings the wolfhounds had to be played by schoolchildren in costume as the dogs themselves were reluctant to show up for state occasions. The last true king to be chosen in this way had been of Lir's family, the Wulfsons, and the line of succession had not been challenged since that time; but now it seemed as though the prince's poor dead father would be the last Wulfson king, as Lir had unsurprisingly failed the wolfhound test that very morning—for the third time in a week—and his father had had no more children with either of his wives.

"Therefore," continued Queen Nimh, "I decree that your birthright as successor to Good King Rufus is forfeit, and the crown shall pass to my own son,

Prince Delbayne of the house of Malygnus. And as Delbayne is of age, he shall be crowned at the coming solstice."

Lir was not upset in the least. He had no wish to be king and had only taken the wolfhound tests at his stepmother's insistence; and so he said, "My stepbrother will make a fine king, Your Majesty. And I will be happy to serve as an apprentice in the royal library. Science and learning are of more interest to me than the crown."

But the queen was not finished.

"According to ancient Lagin law," she continued, "if a man presents himself three times to summon the wolfhounds and fails three times, then that man must leave Lagin forever."

Prince Lir was surprised by the suggestion that he should leave his beloved home, but it was not in his nature to rage and stamp, and so he said respectfully, "I would never even have taken the tests had you not insisted, Your Majesty. And in any case that is, as you say, ancient law and has not been enforced in generations. Not since Prince Faebar the Fallen."

"Thus remembered because he was hurled from the walls into the ocean when he refused to leave the city," Queen Nimh reminded the court. "I have no wish to see you dashed on the rocks, Lir, so you had better leave tonight."

The first to object to this command was Prince Delbayne himself, who had grown up in the same castle as Lir and had ever been his protective older stepbrother.

"Mother," he said, getting to his feet. "My brother has a great many talents that will serve our kingdom better than an ability to commune with wolfhounds."

There is no one in the palace better read. Lir knows every plant in the province and their healing properties. He understands the workings of water, which is undeniably important to a coastal kingdom. Perhaps he cannot build a ship with his own hands, but he can instruct men how to do it. Surely talents such as these must be taken into account."

Many remarked to one another that Delbayne's declaration was an admirable display of friendship and loyalty, but this was not in truth the case. Delbayne was an ambitious and ruthless prince, who had coveted the throne from an early age and had already gone to dark magical extremes to secure the wolf crown for himself. Now he was about to make certain that Lir never returned.

Exile was not enough for Delbayne; he wanted his stepbrother dead.

Fortunately he had his mother on his side.

"My son," said the queen now. "You yourself have summoned the hounds. Many of us here today saw from the battlements how they gathered below you, and therefore you shall be the rightful king. Prince Lir may not covet the throne now, but time may change his mind and there are many who would support his claim. The law may be old, but it is the law. In the name of unity, though it breaks my heart to command it, our beloved Prince Lir must leave Lagin forever."

It was true that after Lir's failed attempt, Delbayne had succeeded in summoning the wolfhounds by the power of his will alone. It had been a strange summoning, as the eyes of the dogs had been as black as river pebbles, something that had never been mentioned in the stories. Stranger still was that when Queen Nimh leaned forward now, emerging from the throne shadow, it seemed as though her eyes had that same glistening quality, and Lir wondered whether she might have succumbed to the lure of dark magic and enchanted the wolfhounds.

The prince was right about the dark magic but wrong about its source. It was Delbayne who had put a spell on both his mother and the hounds so that they would smooth his path to the throne. That very morning, the gathering of half a dozen confused dogs below the Wolfhound's Tooth had effectively crowned the treacherous prince.

Whether there was trickery afoot or not, Lir could see no way to avoid exile without disobeying the queen.

"I will leave as you command, Your Majesty," he said now, bowing low. Though he spoke calmly, Lir was already heartsore at the thought of leaving his beloved Lagin, most especially his friends in the small scientific community who were building a giant spyglass that would enable the watcher to clearly observe the face of the moon.

I will never see the moon clearly, he thought.

"No!" exclaimed Delbayne, and it was here that he played his masterstroke. "There *is* a way that my dear brother Lir may return."

"And what way might that be, my son?" asked the queen.

"Lagin law says a questor knight shall always be granted the shelter of our kingdom and a pension. This law supersedes all."

Again, it seemed to the court that Delbayne was genuinely concerned for the younger prince. If a simple quest could be found for the boy, perhaps one that suited his talents, then he could claim shelter in the

kingdom. The questor knights had been an ancient order whose abbey had been inside the city of Lagin itself and who lived by the very strict code of conduct laid down by the questor charter. Their entire purpose had been to undertake quests for those in need. In these less charitable times, however, the questors had all but disappeared. Good King Rufus, Lir's own father, had been the last questor of note, and Lir still kept one of his father's many golden questor's sashes hanging on his bedpost.

"There haven't been questors in Lagin for many years," snapped Queen Nimh. "I feel certain that there are no quests on the post."

The questing post was a simple totem in the city's main square on which traditionally those in need would nail their requests for help. If a questor knight chose to accept a challenge, he simply claimed the note and tucked it into his questor's sash. In latter times the quests found on the pole were mostly humorous in nature, such as *My dog Bran has been chasing his tail for a year or more without success. If it would please a questor knight to help Bran to catch his tail.*

However, the queen was wrong to assume there were no quests pending. One of the queen's guard, Sir Mug, passed her a note that he had just that moment hastily retrieved from the post. Nimh was irritated by the interruption, but her mood changed as she read the words on the scrap of vellum.

"There *is* a quest, apparently," she said. "It reads as follows: *My daughter Cethlenn was taken by the great dragon Lasvarg to his island. I would have her home safely.*"

A swell of concerned murmurings spread through the hall. Prince Lir was an amiable and useful boy who had repaired many cupboard hinges and sundials throughout the city, and almost no one wanted him devoured by the notoriously heartless Lasvarg. Queen Nimh clearly liked this quest very much, as it seemed certain that the dragon would make short work of a boy like Lir.

"There we have it, then. Will you save Cethlenn, Prince Lir?"

Delbayne had himself posted the note one moonless night not a week ago, but now, as part of his pretense, he made a great show of changing his mind. "Perhaps I misspoke. After all, Lir is a prince, which is a higher rank than knight, so legally speaking he cannot be a questor."

Nimh cut him off. "All princes are by their rank considered questor knights."

Delbayne frowned as though it had not been he who had planted this argument in his mother's mind. "As you say, Mother."

"Exactly," said Queen Nimh. "As I say. Now, Prince Lir, will you leave this place forever or will you seek the shelter of our kingdom by embarking on a quest to save the maiden Cethlenn?"

Lir considered this choice between two horrors. He knew what his father, the questor king, would have chosen, and he would do the same.

"I will accept the quest," he said.

"Very well," said the queen. "Dust off one of your father's old questor's sashes—heaven knows he has no need of them at the bottom of the ocean. Have yourself blessed and then claim this note. You will leave with the tide."

Delbayne hid his face in his hands as a worried and dismayed brother might, but behind those intertwined fingers his smile was broad and triumphant.

It seemed almost inevitable that Lasvarg would eat Prince Lir
alive, but to be sure, the dragon had already been
paid handsomely for the service.

CHAPTER TWO

The Isle of Salt

THE DRAGON LASVARG WOKE ON HIS THRONE DEEP IN THE CAVERNS of the Isle of Salt and remembered when the seat had been draped with a shimmering fleece of gold. The fleece's golden threads had over the years been plucked and sold off for sides of beef or barrels of wine until nothing remained but the yellowed greasy wool of a giant ram. The fleece had been stripped of its glory, like Lasvarg himself, for the dragon was neither feared nor respected in these days of humans, and he rarely ventured out into their world.

For if he did, men would know that dragon fire no longer burned in his chest.

And that they will never know, Lasvarg vowed silently.

The dragon neither flew nor scorched in recent years. Not with his clogged chest and crooked wing. Mostly he coughed in the damp salty air, which he did now, with force.

My days of glory are behind me, he thought miserably. *Once I was the mighty Lasvarg, spewer of dragon flame and amber. Now I am but an instrument of punishment for the crown. I crush enemies of the wolfhound queen and her conniving son. I hold innocent maidens captive and I drown my own objections in wine for reasons I do not understand.*

He was cheered only a little by the sound of Cethlenn the servant girl treading berries in his wine press, which would mean a fresh jug with lunch. The cherry wine reminded him of a more cultured time when dragons ruled the lands from majestic aeries. Days when they had been enlightened overlords with great vaunted halls of art and looming amphitheaters to stage the operas that could last for days. Lasvarg hadn't heard a dragon opera for so long that he had forgotten how they sounded.

At least for the past while he'd had the girl.

She crushes the berries so carefully, he thought.

I am not surprised a prince would come to save her.

His instructions regarding the anticipated questor were quite clear. *Do not preserve the questor prince in dragon amber to be eaten later. Kill him and either eat his corpse or dump the body in the ocean. As you wish.*

The girl he could keep as a servant. She was simply the lure. This made Lasvarg a little happier. The girl made such sweet wine. And something else made him smile a toothy smile.

A questor prince. It had been so very long, and he had always enjoyed the questors and their games. The last fellow had swung at him with an oar. Lasvarg clapped his claws as the memory came back to him.

With a single blast of flame, I burned that oar to kindling in his hands.

And still, with his boat rocking beneath his feet, the questor knight had fought on, his gold sash twinkling.

They had pluck, those questor fellows, Lasvarg thought now. It had indeed been a nobler time.

Which was why the dragon could not help feeling somewhat disappointed when Prince Lir arrived at the cave entrance, looking not at all like the warrior knight the dragon had expected. In fact, had it not been for the prince's sash, Lasvarg might have thought he was simply a young bird fancier come to beg leave to catalog the various gulls and terns that blanketed the Isle of Salt with feathers and droppings.

This stripling could barely lift one of my scales, thought Lasvarg. *There will be nothing interesting about this diversion.*

But the dragon was wrong. Prince Lir would be nothing if not interesting.

· · · · · · · · ·

Lir for his part was not in the least disappointed by his first meeting with the dreaded dragon Lasvarg. The prince considered himself a student of life and was fascinated by the most mundane flower or smallest insect. Nothing was insignificant to Lir; and so, on the supply ferry from Lagin with the stern-faced royal guard hemming him in and a froth of ocean foam bearding his chin, Lir looked forward to his challenge, optimistic that his intelligence and abilities could broker some form of peace with the dragon.

And as he clambered up the stone stairway to the cave entrance, Lir remembered his own father, a questor king, who had thrilled him with bedtime stories of his own youthful quests. Stories that had always ended with the same advice:

The trick to it, Lir my son, the king would say, carrying a candle to the window, *is to work with what is around you.*

Then he would thrust the candle through a gap in the drapes and let the wind extinguish the flame to make his point. It had been many years since his father had been lost at sea, but Lir had never forgotten the lesson.

I must use what is around me, Lir thought now, and he stepped bravely inside the dragon's cave to issue his challenge. The dragon reclined on his throne hewn from the rock, cave rivulets sparkling around his head and the red glint of his eyes casting a glow on his teeth, and Lir was not in the least disappointed.

· · · · · · · · · ·

In the shadow of Lasvarg's wings, the girl Cethlenn trod the berries with some expertise. In Lagin she had been what was known as a cherry orphan, the name given to those children who worked the wine presses from an early age with no pay other than a single meager meal a day and permission to sleep behind the palace kitchens. Cethlenn was considered something of an artist when it came to producing custom batches for specific customers, and she found the labor itself calming. She'd known from the beginning that the dragon would be won over by the sweet wine from Prince Delbayne's own cherry orchard. As she worked now, treading but never stomping, which would bruise the cherries, Cethlenn considered her situation.

Lasvarg has not been such a bad master these past few months, she thought as the cherries squelched between toes permanently stained red by the juice, pulp, and skin. She had known men with more cruelty in their hearts than this dragon could ever have. And she had slept in worse places than this cave.

At least my rock shelf is dry, she thought. *And it is certainly safer sleeping there than on a bed of potato peelings behind the palace kitchens where I had no one to protect me but the wild pups who frequented the yard.*

And so for the moment Cethlenn was content to make the dragon's fine cherry wine and see where the cards might fall with this young questor knight who was supposed to rescue her; as far as Cethlenn was concerned, Prince Delbayne had already rescued her when he'd plucked her from the decaying curls of potato peel and sent her to this place, under royal guard no less, which she'd known even then was curious.

Some royal game is being played out here, she thought. *I will watch closely before I choose my side.*

· · · · · · · · ·

Lasvarg the dragon stood to his full height so that he towered over the prince.

"Why have you come to my lair, boy? Surely not to challenge me?"

Lir opened the folds of his jacket wider so the gold thread of his questor's sash glittered in what little light there was.

"Sir dragon, I come to this place as an official questor, as was my father before me."

Lasvarg's roar echoed through the cave, and the sound was funneled up through the chimney hole far above. "What care I for questors or your father, boy? I will burn you down to rendered fat and swallow you whole in a single slurp."

Lir did not believe the dragon could burn him. It was known in the palace's inner circle that the Lagin dragon had not spewed forth flame for some time. Having said that, Lasvarg would not need fire to kill him.

"Even so," Lir said hurriedly, rummaging in his jacket for the quest contract, "may I present my quest document and suggest that perhaps, since I have traveled so far, you set me the traditional three tasks to perform in exchange for your hostage?"

Lasvarg ignored the contract now being held out to him, glancing instead at Cethlenn. "The servant girl makes my sweet wine, so why should I surrender her to you?"

Lir thought again on his father's advice. "Allow me to suggest the first task. If it does not please you, then we need go no further and you may burn me down to fat and swallow me whole."

Lasvarg was having none of it. "There is nothing you can do for me, boy. I am the stronger of us."

Hastily Lir ventured his first suggestion before Lasvarg could strike him down. "I have noticed that the cave is damp," he said. "And the only thing that prospers in damp is mold. Mold has certain uses as a compress, but in the air it is very dangerous to living things. I can remove the damp and make it easier for you to breathe."

Lasvarg was about to protest that his breathing was fine—wonderful in fact—and he did not need any upstart boy's help with it, but when he drew breath for his protest, his lungs twisted and his body was wracked with shuddering coughs, and by the time he had finished coughing, the questor boy had already begun gathering his materials.

From the rock shelf that served as her bed, chair, and table, Cethlenn watched him work and thought, *This prince might yet live to see another day.*

Lir *did* live to see another day, and three more besides, as he worked on his project. He gathered the dragon's discarded wine casks, and then, dismantling the vessels, he made piles of their planking, nails, and hoops. From these piles he drew the material needed to fashion a system of piping. This he used to construct waterworks that intercepted the main rivulets at the source and ferried the water outdoors, apart from a rainwater stream that he fed into a barrel beside the dragon's throne, to be used as drinking water. And still Lir was not finished. In an old pail he mixed a concoction of seaweed and bird droppings, of which there was an abundant supply, and painted the speckled mush on the patches of mold on the cave walls.

When all this was done, he approached the dragon with the mixture. This was in the late afternoon and Lasvarg was already asleep, and so Lir very gently daubed the dragon's mold-encrusted feet with his brush, careful not to leave any gaps.

When his labors were finished, Lir retired to the surface to pull the splinters from his fingers and found a flat rock suitable for sitting. He set fire to the remainder of the concoction, cooked a fish over the flames, and listened to the waves hiss as they dragged stones into the sea.

After Cethlenn had filled two more jugs with wine for Lasvarg's evening meal, she climbed the stone staircase and sat beside Lir, and he cooked a fish for her.

They spoke of their lives in Lagin, which were as different as two lives could be, though they were much the same age. Lir was surprised to

hear that Cethlenn had no family. Her mother had long since died in the debtors' prison, and even if she had been alive, she never had the skill of writing. So it could not have been she who wrote the quest note.

"Someone is lying to my dear stepbrother Delbayne," said Lir earnestly.

To which Cethlenn laughed and said, "It is true what they say, wolfhound king: *Sometimes the clever ones are the stupid ones.*"

Lir could not argue with being called stupid, for in spite of all his studies, notions, and lofty plans, he often felt that most people marched to a rhythm he could not quite hear, but he could disagree with Cethlenn calling him the wolfhound king.

"Not I," he protested. "Delbayne summoned the wolfhounds and will be crowned king. I do not have the characteristic. In the histories it says that the wolfhound king must be noble and brave, but my father confided in me that any true contender to the throne must share the purest instinct of the wolfhound."

"And what instinct is that?"

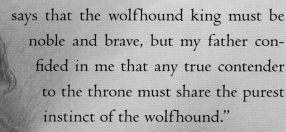

asked Cethlenn with some curiosity; after all, Lagin was built on wolf-hound legends.

"The survival instinct," said Lir. "The true king will summon the wolfhounds when he needs them to survive."

"Did Prince Delbayne need to survive?" she asked.

Lir frowned. "He must have. The secret turmoil of others is not ours to know."

Cethlenn chewed her fish thoughtfully. The only wolfhounds she had ever known were pups who could barely protect her from the palace's angry chefs. She would be in a tight spot indeed if she had to rely on such fluffballs. "The wolfhounds did not save your father," she noted. The entire kingdom knew that King Rufus had perished at sea some years since on a simple fishing trip between quests, leaving Lir's stepmother on the throne.

"Indeed they did not," Lir acknowledged. "But my father was no wolfhound king, and he knew it. Questor knights in general do not have the survival instinct or they would never set off on such dangerous journeys."

And now you are a questor, young prince, Cethlenn thought but did not say.

. . . .

Lasvarg the dreaded dragon slept on, and while he slept, Lir's poultice did its healing work drying out the mold; what's more, it sent spores deep into the dragon's veins, healing Lasvarg's tainted blood and drying out his lungs. The dragon dreamed an entire opera and woke refreshed but unsettled by the unfamiliar feeling of well-being.

I have been placed under an enchantment, he thought, and sprang to his feet. Feet which no longer pained him.

"What sorcery is this?" he cried, then automatically flared his nostrils to draw in the deep breath of air needed to unleash an excoriating plume of dragon flame. But he stopped himself in time; it would have been mortifying to snort nothing but air and dust, and also the boy was standing before him. The little questor with his gold sash.

"No sorcery, sir dragon," the boy said. "Simply a mold remedy. This chamber is clear, but I see there is a smaller chamber in the deeper shadows, so perhaps tomorrow—"

"No," said Lasvarg sternly. "Leave the dark chamber be. That room is for me alone. You may consider your first task completed to my satisfaction."

Prince Lir was delighted. "That is wonderful news. If you are satisfied, then under questor rules we may proceed to my second task. And if I may be so bold, there is a service I feel I could perform for you, should you be brave enough to take the journey with me."

From high up on the cave walls where she was tugging weed from rock crevices, Cethlenn called down, "Challenging my master in this manner is big talk for a small fellow."

Lasvarg puffed his chest out with some effort. "Brave enough, is it? Brave now, you say, questor? Was I not brave enough to sink the Persian Armada that still lies rotting on the beach? Was Lasvarg the dread fire lizard not sufficiently brave to decimate an entire legion of Northmen? I burned those warriors down to statues. Have you never visited the site? Those figures stand as a testament to my bravery."

Prince Lir seemed oblivious to the fact that he was about to be squashed under the feet he had so recently cleared of mold and instead continued to make his case for a second task.

"My father, who was a questor before me, often said that there were many forms of bravery."

Lasvarg typically despised this type of vague statement.

"How many forms?" he thundered. "And which specific one would I need to take this so-called journey with you?"

"Trust," said Lir simply. "You would need to trust me."

Lasvarg the dragon was so stunned he began to laugh, and without so much effort now that there was no damp in his chest. "Trust!" he scoffed. "Trust a *human*? Have you lost your mind, boy? Trust is not a real thing. It was invented for storybooks so children might believe their lives would end happily ever after. You are a fool, prince. And now I must eat you."

Lir did not flinch but instead asked the looming creature, "Before you eat me, sir dragon, might I tell you why you would need to trust me?"

Lasvarg raised a scaly foot, fully the size of Lir himself, over the prince's head and growled, "Tell me."

Lir told the dragon his plan and the dragon said, "Ridiculous. The very idea is impossible. It could never work."

Lir shrugged. "It can be done, and there is no obligation on your part until the third task is completed. It is a lot for you to endure, but the rewards would be truly magnificent. As a student of the natural world, I would myself relish the opportunity to observe."

Lasvarg's anger lost its heat, and the dragon sat on his throne noticing that the chair was not slick with cave water as it had been only the previous day.

"Leave me," he ordered. "Go and cook fish.

We will speak more tomorrow."

CHAPTER THREE

The Burning Scale

ON THE ISLAND'S STONY
beach, Lir set about
gathering more dried
seaweed and gull drop-
pings for the fire he
would build in his
pail. He was about
to crack his tinder
stones together when
Cethlenn joined him
on the flat rock that
had become their bench.
"The bird-dropping
kindling gives the fish an
unpleasant flavor," she remarked.
"Perhaps you might try this?"

She handed Lir a bronze-colored disc that he realized was a dragon scale, and his scientist's heart skipped a beat. A dragon scale for fuel? How fascinating.

Lir rinsed his pail, then tossed in the scale.

It took several cracks of the stones for the scale to catch fire, but when it finally did, the flames were soft without even a strand of blue and the odor was rich like clover honey.

"Lasvarg has a fiery heart," observed Cethlenn. "Even the scales he sheds can burn for hours."

The fish tasted sweet that evening, and Lir thought that if he ever had to choose a last meal, he would have the same meal in the same company.

· · · · · · · · ·

The next morning, Lir was woken by a shadow falling across his face. The dragon Lasvarg stood between him and the rising sun.

"Tell me how it would be done," ordered the dragon, gesturing with his one functioning wing. And so Lir rose and explained the procedure, and how he had performed it once before on a hawk who had misjudged the fighting prowess of a rabbit.

Lasvarg nodded as he listened but was still not satisfied. "Draw it," he instructed. "In the sand."

They found a patch of sand and Lir sketched out his proposal with a stick. Cethlenn crept outside and watched while the young prince worked, and she found that for the first time in her short, hard life she would like it if someone who was not useful to her could stay alive.

· · · · · · · · · ·

Lir labored for three days on the pulley and
weight, salvaging an anchor, its winch, and
its chain from the wreckage of a Persian ship
on the southern rocks. Cethlenn was given
leave to help him splice tattered lengths of
rope into coils of sufficient length.

Lasvarg himself agreed to carry the anchor across the island to his cave, muttering, "I don't know why I bother. This will not work, and you'll most likely be dead tomorrow."

Lir felt the shadow of these comments shroud his heart but he labored on, and as his machine neared completion, Lasvarg's threats dried up and the dragon threw his weight behind the task, even taking instruction without complaint. As the three worked, Cethlenn sang a song she had learned at her mother's knee, which went as follows:

"The mountains fall into the sea,
And men will chop down every tree.
But men will live and men will die,
Yet dragons ever rule the sky.
Doom doom, dragon's doom,
Feel the wind a-rushing by.
Doom doom, dragon's doom,
Dragons ever rule the sky."

Even Lasvarg was grunting along by the third day.

On the third night, Lasvarg
heard the wings of a bird flap in the cave's chimney hole.
This was unusual because normally gulls did not dare to approach the
cave, but Lasvarg had been expecting this particular bird and so climbed
to the cave ceiling, where he found a raven waiting.

The raven was bloodied and battered from its long journey and also
from a squabble with some of the island's fiercely territorial seagulls.
No bird would have made such a perilous trip unless enchanted.

"Caw?" it croaked to Lasvarg.

Lasvarg knew what Prince Delbayne wished to know. *When will you
kill him?*

The dragon was irritated by the raven, but also by the impudent
prince whom he had chosen to serve. *Why do I follow this human's orders?*
thought the dragon now. *I can't remember.*

"Soon," he said to the bird, then he bared his teeth to frighten it away.

. . . .

Lasvarg awoke to the sound of Cethlenn's press churning as she prepared his cherry wine. It was early for the girl to be at her labors, but he would need the wine for what was to come. The boy Lir had winched the anchor high overhead, and it swayed slightly from the journey. Now that the moment had actually arrived, Lasvarg was suddenly nervous, an unsettling feeling for a dragon, which made him more nervous.

Lir stepped onto the throne's dais and asked, "Are you ready, sir dragon?"

Lasvarg gave serious thought to abandoning the entire ridiculous enterprise. He could simply do what he had already been paid to do and go back to his drab life, but in sending the raven, Delbayne had made a serious error. He had reminded Lasvarg that his life was one of servitude.

When once I saw this land from above and listened to opera, the dragon thought.

"Yes, boy," he said. "I am ready."

. . . .

Lir explained the procedure one final time as he strapped Lasvarg into the brace.

"For many years I have studied birds, their wings in particular. Once, as I mentioned, I nursed an injured hawk back to health."

Lasvarg grimaced as his bent wing was cranked out to its full span. "I am no bird, boy."

Lir tied off the strap. "No. But the skeletal structure of your wing is similar. From my observations I would say you fractured your wing some time ago."

"I did that," Lasvarg said, then turned his head away. "Wrestling a seal who was to be my dinner. A tiny fellow, smaller than you, but look what he did."

But was that what had really happened? Or was that the story Lasvarg told himself?

"The wing has healed incorrectly and cannot bear the burden of flight. So if you are to fly again, sir dragon . . ."

"You must break the bone and reset it."

"Precisely," said Lir.

Cethlenn handed Lasvarg a jug of her cherry wine. "This is stronger than ever before, my lord," she said. "To help with the pain."

Lasvarg took a long draft and winced. "Strong indeed."

"And one last instruction," said Lir. "No wine while you recover."

"Of course," grumbled Lasvarg. "Why have any pleasures at all when I can allow humans to break my bones? I must be mad."

"My lord," said Cethlenn, "you are not mad. I trust the word of this prince, and perhaps you are of the same mind."

"Humph," Lasvarg said, and took another swig of wine.

· · · · · · · ·

The procedure was straightforward enough. Cethlenn was tasked with striking a pin from the winch, which would release the sharpened anchor, which should then slice Lasvarg's flesh and pulverize the badly healed knot of bone. Lir would go quickly to work and set the bones together, stitch the wound, and splint the lot with barrel planks held in place with nails hammered directly into the bone. It would be an extreme test of the dragon's fortitude, but should he hold his nerve, then the eventual rewards would make one of his dearest dreams come true.

He would fly again.

Lir washed his hands in a bucket of salt water and then asked, "Are you ready, sir dragon?"

"I am," said Lasvarg. "But know something, boy: if this is trickery, then I shall tear the wing from my own body and hunt you down."

Lir was puzzled. "But I am a questor, sir dragon, and a scientist. Trickery is not in my nature."

Still Lasvarg was not convinced, but the dream of flight had taken hold of him. "Strike the pin," he told Cethlenn.

The maiden knocked the wooden pin from its groove. Freed, the anchor whistled down and smashed through the dragon's wing.

. . . .

Lasvarg was not fully awake during the procedure; the pain was so great that he was forced to retreat from it into the haze of his own mind. A part of him fled to the past and the memories of his own kind when they were mighty rulers with towers of learning and fleets of airships to ferry them over the oceans. Another part of the dragon could feel the questor Lir beavering at the white-hot source of his pain. He heard the scrape of his broken bone and the clangs of the hammer and thought, *What have I done? The human is murdering me!*

For this was a greater pain than he had ever known.

And then there was a cool hand on his brow and a gentle voice singing him a lullaby.

"All of those who have gone before,
Father, mother, brother, more.
Our stories, they are yours to keep.
We wait for you in the land of sleep."

The maiden knows my very thoughts, mused Lasvarg,
and he sank into a deep slumber.

CHAPTER FOUR

The Dark Chamber

TWO MORE RAVENS VISITED THE CAVE BUT NEITHER RECEIVED AN audience with the dragon, who slumbered on, sprawled across his throne, kept warm by a fleece scrubbed clean of its greasy sheen by Prince Lir.

Some days later, Cethlenn and the boy sat aboveground on their bench waiting for Lasvarg to awaken and were surprised to see a wolf-hound plodding up from the surf, exhausted.

"He must have fallen overboard in the straits," guessed Lir. "Surely no hound could swim the distance from Lagin."

By the following evening, there were two more hounds panting on the beach.

"Did you summon them?" teased Cethlenn. "Perhaps you are the wolfhound king after all."

Lir shook his head. "Not I. Three times I failed the test."

"I had thought those tests were just for ceremony," said Cethlenn.

"I too believed this," admitted Lir. "But it seems that the queen takes ancient law very seriously."

Cethlenn dipped her feet in the surf and was surprised to see the red cherry dye already fading after only a few days. "Perhaps not, but you do have a pure heart, Lir." And then she changed the subject. "I can't remember the last time I had a day without work," she said.

"A day with a friend." Lir smiled, and he cooked a fish for her. Cethlenn remarked that the fish tasted of clover honey.

Many days they spent in each other's company while the dragon healed. Cethlenn taught Lir her songs, and how to coax winkles from their shells, and which nooks held the richest treasures of gulls' eggs. Lir for his part tended to the sleeping dragon and cooked honey fish.

In later times, when he was a different person, Lir would dream of these days and awaken with tears upon his cheeks.

. . . .

One evening when the meal was over, Lir declared that he would change the seaweed dressing on Lasvarg's wing and left Cethlenn alone with the wolfhounds, who were always nearby these days. She was not in the least afraid and in fact thought she recognized a spoon-shaped marking on the snout of the largest dog.

Is it possible? she thought. *Could it be one of my potato peel pups grown to a hound?*

"Is it you, Spoon?" she asked the dog. "Did you miss me?"

In response, the dog who may or may not have been Spoon turned its back, which Cethlenn took to mean that the wolfhound had no interest in her; but any dog person could have told her that a good wolfhound turns its back to watch for intruders.

This dog was guarding Cethlenn.

· · · · · · · · ·

During the fourth week, when Lasvarg finally awoke, Lir began to suspect that dragons healed at an accelerated rate. His bones had already expelled the nails hammered into them and shrugged off the splints.

"This feels worse than before, boy," the dragon grumbled when the sleep mist cleared. "I should squash you like a rodent. Bring me some wine."

"No wine," said Lir sternly. "Wine slows healing and cherries suppress magic. You are a magical creature, so cherry wine is the worst thing for you."

"Food, then," demanded the dragon. "For I am famished. None of your white fish, either. I need red meat."

"I could hunt for a seal?" offered Lir.

Lasvarg laughed, then immediately grimaced in pain. "Ha! No, princeling, the seals in these waters have devoured bigger morsels than you, and I need my physician. I have meat stored in the dark chamber, but it is preserved in dragon amber and I have not had the flame to melt it just recently." Lasvarg fell into a moody silence then, for he had never spoken aloud the fact that he no longer had dragon flame.

I might have a surprise for you soon, thought Lir, but he did not say so to the dragon as his theory was just a theory at that moment.

"I will make you a meal fit for a dragon lord," he said instead, for yet another idea had struck him. "Wait here."

Lasvarg raised his healing wing with some effort.

"That was my plan," he murmured, and closed his eyes again for a recuperative sleep that could possibly stretch over several days.

· · · · · · · · ·

Lir's idea was this: If dragon scales burned with such fierce heat, then perhaps they could melt dragon amber, a kind of preservative resin with which dragons slathered their prey so it would not turn. There were dozens of scales scattered around the cave, and he could easily select one of the smaller carcasses to drag from the dark chamber. The prince knew he had been forbidden to enter, but he felt Lasvarg would forgive him this minor disobedience, especially if the dragon regained the power of flight.

· · · · · · · · ·

Leaving the main cave behind, Prince Lir followed a golden glow along a narrow passage until the floor grew slick and the cold crept through the soles of his boots and along his limbs.

The perfect larder, thought Lir. *Food will stay fresh in here forever.*

The passage was oppressive to be sure, with its unevenly tilted walls and the layers of shadows that jumped and reared in the glow from the distant amber. It occurred to Lir that Lasvarg's belly must scrape the rock floor to fit in the space.

Onward, he thought to himself, ignoring a feeling of foreboding that clawed at his own stomach.

Down the tunnel Lir continued, testing the ground with each step till the narrow space opened to form a low cavern littered with crystals of amber. Inside, each was a carcass of some beast or other that had been hunted by Lasvarg and stored for winter consumption. Smaller crystals contained rabbits or fish and larger ones contained goats, sharks, and even a small whale.

Most people would have felt revulsion at such a macabre sight, but Lir the scientist saw only the possibilities.

If dragon amber could be somehow re-created, entire villages could live through the winter, he marveled.

The prince tucked his questor's sash into his belt so that it would not become tarnished and began to sort through the crystals. The dragon's favorite dish was seal meat, so this was what Lir sought now.

But the prince did not find a seal, for he was distracted by a flash of gold in the depths of one amber crystal. A man-size crystal.

Lir righted the crystal with a heave and squinted through the amber haze. He saw that the gold was a questor's sash like his own and the man wearing it was his own father, preserved perfectly as he had been in life apart from the deep slashes that cut through his sash and the flesh below.

Lir's breath caught in his throat.

Not lost at sea, then, he thought, and his heart slowly hardened like a tiny amber crystal.

Murdered by Lasvarg.

Everything was clear now, and Lir could no longer pretend to himself that the house of Malygnus was innocent in all of this. Either the queen or Prince Malygnus himself had employed the dragon to murder his father. *And I suppose I am to be next,* he thought.

And for the first time in his life it seemed as though science and knowledge were inconsequential. Lir's mind was overpowered by his heart, and he stormed from the cavern.

CHAPTER FIVE

The Third Task

CETHLENN FOUND LIR AMONG THE PERSIAN WRECKS ON THE island's southern coast, with legions of gulls watching him from the masts, spars, and rotting rigging. Lir was busy in the bowels of a narrow boat, tearing out what could not be saved.

"You saw something in the dark chamber?" she called to him from the shore, and the growing pack of wolfhounds ranging along the waterline raised a howling at the sound of her voice. If Lir had been himself, he might have noticed that Cethlenn casually silenced them with a wave of her hand.

"I saw something," he said, tearing a rotten plank free in a shower of splinters. "Something terrible, and now I must leave."

Cethlenn climbed into the hull and sat on the remains of a bench. "Have you forgotten the third task?"

"'Tis done," said Lir. "Though your master does not know it yet." He paused in his frantic labors and sat beside her. "So you are free to come with me, Cethlenn. If you wish it."

Cethlenn took his hand. She could not even consider returning to Lagin.

Cethlenn felt safe on the island and was not ready to sacrifice that for a prince whom she feared would shortly be dead, though she certainly did not wish him so. Quite the opposite.

"I wish for you to stay here with me. I am feeling something, Lir. Happiness, perhaps, though I cannot tell, having never known it."

"I had hoped to stay," admitted Lir. "We two, with the dragon. But now that dream is ruined. So I must return to Lagin and learn the truth."

"Why must you go?" Cethlenn asked. "You never wished to be king."

"That is true," he agreed. "But I do wish for a good king. The people of Lagin deserve that much."

Cethlenn let go of his hand. "Perhaps someday when they have a good king who cares for the poor, I will return to Lagin, Lir," she said. "But that time has not yet come."

Lir nodded. Of course he understood. "I will come back, and then I shall ask you once more to come with me to Lagin."

"If you survive, prince, please do come back," said Cethlenn. "Ask me once more."

Lir returned to his labors. He would build a light boat with a shallow draft and fly over the waves to Lagin to confront his stepbrother.

· · · · · · · · ·

Lir could not have known that there was no need for him to labor on his boat, as Prince Delbayne was already gathering his magic to visit the Isle of Salt—for it is not in the nature of powerful men to let potential rivals simply live free.

When Delbayne's ravens returned to Lagin without a reply from the dragon Lasvarg, Delbayne knew that something was amiss and so assembled a squadron of his hardiest royal soldiers for the trip.

The guards were already loyal to him, so there was no need for enchantment there; he saved this for his growing pack of wolfhounds. The dark path to which Delbayne had pledged his soul was ancient, powerful, and forbidden, and there were perhaps only a dozen skilled masters in the known world. Of these Delbayne was certainly the youngest.

This was an adaptation of Druids' magic and was known as blood magic, for that was the price it demanded: the practitioner's very lifeblood. The sorcerer could live on without his blood, but he would be less human for it, which bothered Delbayne not in the least. Delbayne drew vials of his own blood every day, each one infused with strands of his own power, and used them to infect soldiers, nobles, wolfhounds, and even his own mother, Queen Nimh. The humans he bent to his will and the wolfhounds he locked in cages so they would be murderously hungry by the time they were needed and would without question attack whosoever Delbayne ordered them to. In this case his own stepbrother, Prince Lir.

· · · · · · · · ·

On the shores of the Isle of Salt, Lir labored on, weaving ropes from sturdy strands and cutting sound patches of canvas from the hearts of rotting sails, and after several days had a sail for his boat. He rolled the boat to the water's edge on a system of logs and sat on the wooden cross bench waiting for the wind to change.

And as he waited, Lasvarg came to see him, though not on foot as he might have done a week previously but carried by the strength of his own wings, the beating of which set dust and smaller stones whirling around Lir like a sandstorm. On any other day the prince would have been truly jubilant that his operation had been a success. But not today.

"Leave me to my work, sir dragon," the young man called to the sky as he sawed a thick hank of rope with a blade that had originally served as the spike on a Persian helmet. "Leave me or kill me as you did my father."

Lasvarg landed on a rocky outcrop some small distance away and coughed to relieve a small irritation in his throat.

"The questor knight. He was your father. I see now. He fought valiantly. I want you to know that he was the one who broke my wing with a mighty swing from his oar. No mean feat for a man on the deck of a boat."

"You murdered him nonetheless. Bravery notwithstanding."

Lasvarg shrugged. "Prince Delbayne gave me my orders and I obeyed."

"I see," said Lir, sawing at the rope with renewed vigor. "I did not realize that Lasvarg the mighty dragon took assassination orders from humans."

Lasvarg found that he could not remember events clearly. "He arrived some years ago with a shipment of wine, long before Cethlenn was sent to press cherries for me. And since that shipment I have done his bidding. But now I am wondering why, so I will take neither wine nor commands from Prince Delbayne from here on out."

Lir had a thought, but it was too late for ideas. His heart was broken and quests seemed suddenly unimportant.

"No matter, sir dragon," he said. "I am leaving. You may kill me if you wish, since you care not for the strict rules of questing."

"It is you who does not care for the rules," Lasvarg countered. "We have a contract and in that contract there are three tasks. You have completed but two."

Lir challenged this. "Three!" he shouted. "I have completed three, for now that the mold and wine are leaving your system, your amber will return and therefore your flames. It is only a matter of time. And then perhaps you would do me the favor of not using your fire against questors."

Lasvarg was stunned, for he realized then that Prince Lir spoke the truth. His flames would return; now he remembered that the scratching in his throat was a tiny spark that would ignite the amber that his body had always produced.

"Lir," he said, confused by his tangled history with Lagin's monarchy. "You must stay. We can repair this situation."

The questor prince sighed, for he was sad to leave and suspected that the dragon had not been responsible for his own actions for a long while, but leave he must. Delbayne had questions to answer, even if asking them would surely get Lir killed.

"I must go," he said. "I will return for Cethlenn if she will have me. But for now I must confront my stepbrother."

Suddenly Cethlenn appeared on the rise and called down to youth and dragon. "A ship!" she said.

And at that moment, the wolfhounds set up an echoing howl that spread in a chain out to sea, where it was taken up by a pack of dogs on the ship itself.

Lasvarg flapped his wings and rose on the wind the better to see the craft that was approaching his isle.

"It seems as though we shall both have our confrontation," he cried.

CHAPTER SIX

Blood Magic

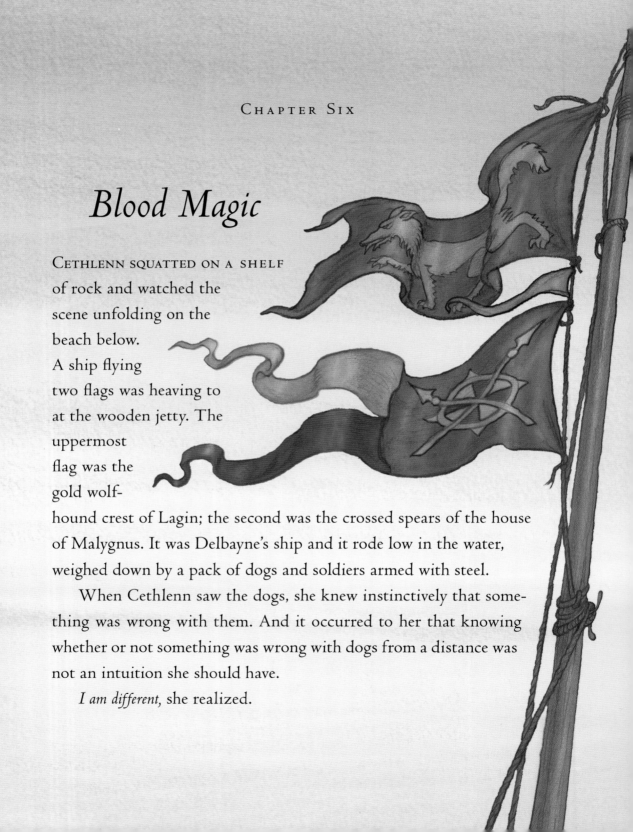

CETHLENN SQUATTED ON A SHELF
of rock and watched the
scene unfolding on the
beach below.
A ship flying
two flags was heaving to
at the wooden jetty. The
uppermost
flag was the
gold wolf-
hound crest of Lagin; the second was the crossed spears of the house
of Malygnus. It was Delbayne's ship and it rode low in the water,
weighed down by a pack of dogs and soldiers armed with steel.

When Cethlenn saw the dogs, she knew instinctively that something was wrong with them. And it occurred to her that knowing
whether or not something was wrong with dogs from a distance was
not an intuition she should have.

I am different, she realized.

She'd always suspected this but knew that most people considered themselves different in one way or another, and so she had discounted the thought and got on with the business of surviving the Lagin backstreets. But she could ignore this suspicion no longer, because now it was rising from the depths of her mind and threatening to overwhelm her.

As she gazed at the ship of tainted dogs, Cethlenn felt her own shoulder blades rise like the hackles of the wolfhounds who had become her guardians. She patted the hound nearest her, the one she was now sure was indeed Spoon, the pup she remembered once yipping at strangers in the yard behind the palace kitchens, where she'd slept. Spoon pressed his head against her hand so that she could feel the shape of his skull. The hound's hackles rose and Cethlenn's fingers slid naturally between his shoulder blades as if they belonged there.

Cethlenn felt herself drift away, daydreaming but with more purpose, as though her mind was drifting somewhere specific. She noticed a heat shimmer in the air even though it was not overly warm, and her vision changed, becoming sharper and more saturated with color. And there was a girl before her, stroking her head.

That is me, she realized, but she was not shocked by this. *I am looking at myself through Spoon's eyes.*

Why was this happening? Could she be the wolfhound king—or queen, rather? Surely not. Lir had told her that the survival instinct brought about a summoning. But she had been in tighter spots before and never felt such a communion with the wolfhounds.

Cethlenn directed Spoon's gaze toward the jetty and saw the soldiers disembark and approach Lir, and then she understood why this was happening now.

It is not my own survival that concerns me.

. . . .

Prince Delbayne and his cohort disembarked and headed toward the cave where they expected to find Lasvarg, but veered off when they saw the dragon perched upon a high rock by the stony beach. Lir noticed that while the royal soldiers seemed understandably nervous about approaching a dragon, Delbayne had no such hesitation and strode directly toward the armada graveyard.

"Do you see what you have made me do, dragon?" he said. "I must finish a task for which you have already been paid."

Perhaps Delbayne was expecting Lasvarg to

react with meek contrition, but this was not what happened.

"I think you forget your place, boy!" roared the dragon. "Perhaps you have also forgotten what it is I have done for you and could easily do *to* you."

Delbayne took a step back, for it was obvious that Lasvarg could crush the prince simply by stepping down from his perch, yet he was far from cowed.

"You can do nothing but what I tell you, lizard," he sneered. "Hold your tongue lest I decide you are of no further use to me."

From his concealed position on the deck of his boat, Prince Lir was seething with anger and thought himself a fool that he had ever considered Delbayne a friend. The same man that he felt certain had ordered the murder of his father. And now he had come to finish the task that Lasvarg would not: the murder of Lir himself.

"Is it blood magic, brother?" he asked, climbing over the boat's keel onto the beach.

Delbayne was not surprised to see his stepbrother. "The sea air has cleared your mind, Lir. For years you have swallowed my every falsehood, and yet you spend a month on this island and you see clearly."

Lir felt the urge to attack there and then, despite only having a pathetic helmet spike for a weapon, but first there were more truths to be gleaned.

"You bewitched the wolfhounds for the summoning, and the mighty Lasvarg to clear your path, and your own mother to smooth the way."

Delbayne smiled contemptuously. "Dear mother," he said. "She loves you, you know. It was impressive how she fought the magic, but in the end, everyone succumbs. She will place the wolfhound crown on my head in less than a week."

"I did wonder how it was done," continued Lir. "But now it is obvious. It was the cherries from your precious orchard."

Delbayne clapped his hands. "Well done, Prince Lir. You have finally put your mind to good use. Of course it was the cherries. The cherry tree roots feed upon the very blood from these veins. The cost is great but the rewards are so much greater, for see what my magic has brought me: the very throne of Lagin itself."

Lir nodded. Blood magic was powerful, dark, and forbidden. Most who attempted to master it died in the process, but Delbayne had evidently been using it from an early age and was surely a powerful sorcerer to have not only survived but thrived.

"That crown is not yet yours, brother," warned Lir.

There would be some form of battle here, of that there was no doubt, but Lir could not tell exactly what form it would take or even what side the dragon would fight on. His might would be the deciding factor. Delbayne had his royal guard and his enchanted hounds, but they would be as insects to the dragon, especially now that his wing had healed. There was also the matter of the hounds who had made the swim from Lagin, though they seemed to have disappeared from the beach.

"Before we begin, I should tell you that Lasvarg has not tasted your wine in some time," Lir revealed. "He has broken that ruinous habit."

"Just as your father broke his wing," sneered Delbayne. "King Rufus was truly a mighty warrior. A shame the dragon killed him."

"*You* killed him," Lir spat. "The dragon was merely your instrument."

Lasvarg had not spoken since his initial outburst of defiance, for he was trapped in a place between his own will and that of Prince Delbayne. The blood magic was weaker than it had been in years, yet still it held him in thrall.

"Look at him," taunted Delbayne. "The dreaded dragon Lasvarg. I shall not even call on him this day. My bloodhounds shall do his work. Farewell, *brother* Lir."

And with a click of his finger, Delbayne unleashed his hounds, who sprang forward as one in a growling, slavering pack of teeth and claws.

Lir knew that all his thoughts and plans counted for nothing in the face of such savagery, and he deeply regretted that he had not arrived at this island earlier and forged a deeper friendship with Cethlenn and perhaps even freed Lasvarg completely from his bonds.

The wolfhounds will tear me limb from limb, he thought sadly. *I who was once destined to be their king.*

But the enchanted wolf-hounds did not tear Prince Lir apart,

for their force was met by a greater one. The hounds who had come from the ocean countered their attack with one of their own, and while Delbayne's dogs were vicious, they were also stupefied by enchantment and no match for the clear-eyed wolfhounds who flowed down from the rise, their coats streaming behind them like battle pennants.

Someone runs the hounds, Lir realized.

Though there had always been tales of a magical warrior who was pure of heart and could control the wolfhounds without so much as a whistle, no living person had ever seen a true wolfhound king.

Perhaps this was because the next wolfhound king was actually a queen. She had been on the Isle of Salt, her magic suppressed by the dye in Delbayne's blood cherries, which had coated her from toes to thighs. But Cethlenn had not pressed cherry wine for weeks.

As all of this dawned on Lir, he swung around to see Cethlenn, her teeth bared, sweeping through the possessed dogs like a dervish, made fierce by the wolfhound spirit.

She is the wolfhound queen, he thought. *My wolfhound queen.*

Delbayne felt a shadow flit across his heart as he too realized the truth. The legends were true and the wolfhound warrior was real. He cursed himself for inadvertently keeping her alive and then turned his mind to the task at hand. His priority had changed, that much was clear. Cethlenn was the target now, for she was the rightful heir to the throne of Lagin.

"Kill the girl!" he ordered his royal guard. "At all costs she must die!"

His soldiers attacked in a tight phalanx, yet they were unfortunate in that Lasvarg, still wrestling with the blood magic, tumbled from his rock at that moment and knocked them aside like wooden pins. Lasvarg too was unfortunate, as the tumble peeled back his armored scales and a poisoned spear pierced through to the flesh below, its head snapping off and beginning a decades-long journey toward the dragon's heart.

However, the pain cleared Lasvarg's mind of the final blood cherry residue, and he rose with a mighty flap of his wings and loomed above the melee in all his terrible glory. The soldiers who could run did so, hell-for-leather back toward the ship with the assorted hounds close on their tails.

In spite of the fact that Lasvarg was now undoubtedly free of his magical restraints, Delbayne focused his attention on Cethlenn.

"*I* shall be king!" he raged. "I *am* king!"

He gathered his dark magic for one death strike, and a haze of roiling smoke shot through with black lightning gathered around his fist. The smoke took the form of an arrowhead, the point of which was aimed directly at Cethlenn's heart.

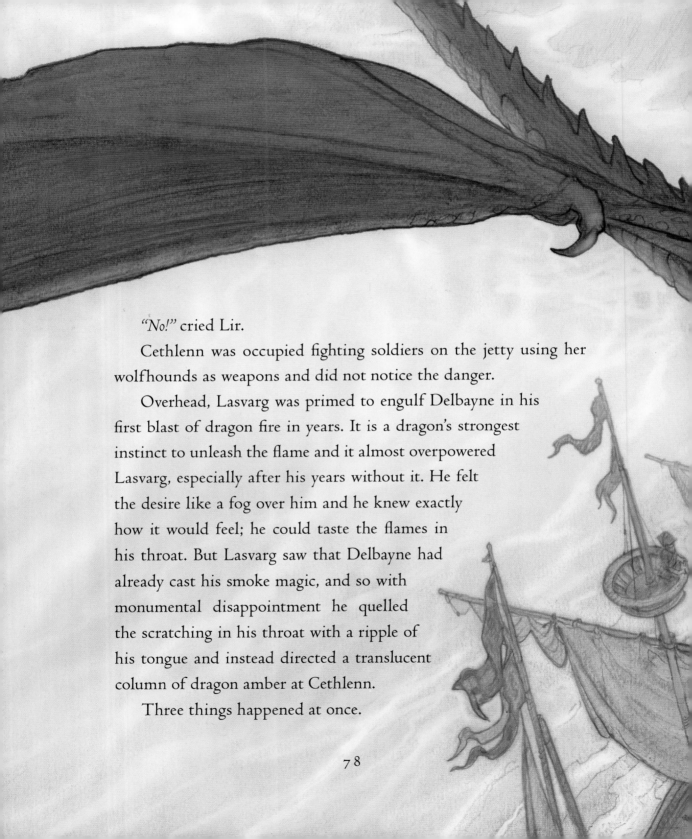

"*No!*" cried Lir.

Cethlenn was occupied fighting soldiers on the jetty using her wolfhounds as weapons and did not notice the danger.

Overhead, Lasvarg was primed to engulf Delbayne in his first blast of dragon fire in years. It is a dragon's strongest instinct to unleash the flame and it almost overpowered Lasvarg, especially after his years without it. He felt the desire like a fog over him and he knew exactly how it would feel; he could taste the flames in his throat. But Lasvarg saw that Delbayne had already cast his smoke magic, and so with monumental disappointment he quelled the scratching in his throat with a ripple of his tongue and instead directed a translucent column of dragon amber at Cethlenn.

Three things happened at once.

Lasvarg's spew of amber coated Cethlenn, repelling Delbayne's poisonous cloud. And while Delbayne was gathering power for a second assault, Lir reached the conclusion that there was no peaceful solution to be found here and, almost without a thought as to what he was actually doing, stepped forward, lifted the Persian helmet spike that he still held in his hands, and buried the makeshift knife in his stepbrother's chest.

It was a mortal wound that no amount of sorcery could heal.

Delbayne fell back on the beach, grasping at the blood-slickened spike.

"I shall never be king," he said, and with that realization Delbayne became more powerful than he had ever been, for it is in that moment before death that the black magician's true might rises to the surface unhindered by expectations, uncertainties, or any lingering sense of right or wrong. Delbayne looked deep inside himself to fashion a hex that would endure long after he had departed this world.

With the full weight of his mortal energies and white-hot hatred behind him, Delbayne drew on the dark powers of the earth, inscribing complex pictograms in the air with black light, speaking in a tongue alien to boy and dragon, who both now leaned over the dying prince.

"I curse you," Delbayne spat. "Until the dragon's dying day you shall both lose everything you love."

Lasvarg was unimpressed. "You babble, prince. Better for you to beg this boy's forgiveness than hurl curses."

There were red bubbles on Delbayne's lips, and a great pallor crept up from his neck.

"I curse you both," he said, and died.

Lir saw that he had Delbayne's blood on his hands.

"What does that portend?" he asked Lasvarg fearfully. "That we are to lose everything we love?"

Lasvarg winced, holding his side where the spear had pierced his flank. "Nothing. He was raving, that is all."

"Cethlenn," said Lir then, wasting not another second on the dead prince. "You must free her, sir dragon."

Lasvarg knew that only he could liberate the girl from her cocoon of dragon amber, and he would do so with a blast of the fire he so longed to unleash. Never had the cause been so noble.

"Indeed," he said. "It shall be done."

Boy and dragon sped to where Cethlenn stood encased in amber that had flowed under her toes and solidified in ripples.

Lir pressed his face against the warm crystal. "Quickly, sir dragon, before the amber crushes her."

"No," said Lasvarg. "The amber will not crush the girl. Fresh meat stays fresh and live meat stays alive inside dragon amber. I melted a salmon from a block after a hundred years and it jumped into my mouth."

Lir winced, thinking of his own father in the cave who had been mortally wounded before being preserved, but tried to concentrate on this girl whose name he could not recall at this moment but who he knew was important to him.

"You must try," he begged.

"I shall indeed try," said the dragon, stretching his neck, mindful that he must be careful with his flame, eager as he was to unleash it. Too much would melt the girl; not enough would slowly heat the amber, cooking her inside.

Lasvarg opened his jaws until they cracked, which set sparks dancing at the back of his throat, and he thought, *At last. The flame.*

But no flame flowed from the dragon, nothing but a dry whoosh of air. Again Lasvarg tried, and perhaps the air was slightly warmer this time, but there was certainly no flame. A dozen more times Lasvarg tried, each with more desperation, but by the end even the tinder sparks in his throat had been extinguished, and it was clear what was happening.

The curse. I am losing what I love, he thought in anguish. *My dragon flame.*

"Delbayne!" roared the dragon, and he turned on the dead prince as though he would rend him limb from limb, but the sorcerer's body had already been consumed by dark magic and was nothing more than an oil stain on the beach.

Lir too was losing what he loved.

Cethlenn.

First her name went, and then the very sight of her, as all he could see before him now was a cloudy crystal obelisk.

This was not all the curse cost Lir, for he lost the very essence of himself. His notions and ideas left him, and in their turn the memories on which these ideas were built. All these sparks in his mind were extinguished just as surely as Lasvarg's flame.

And now as he turned, he saw there was a dragon by his side.

"Why do you howl, sir dragon?" he asked. "Are you hungry?"

Lasvarg found himself glaring at an oil slick on a stony beach with no memory of his beloved island or what he was doing here. And now this youth was asking whether or not he was hungry.

"If I were hungry, boy," he replied gruffly, "how would you prevent me from sating that hunger on your flesh?"

Lir thought about this, and the best his impoverished mind could come up with was "I would stand in a rock pool and perhaps catch a salmon in my hands."

"Be quick about it, then," demanded Lasvarg, "and it is possible I will not eat you after all."

Lir did not catch a salmon but he did manage to throttle a seagull that was trapped in an old fishing net. In fact, it seemed to Lir that the coastline was something of a maritime graveyard, littered with the listing carcasses of rotting ships and armored plates.

"I shall call you Gull, because you do not seem to have a name," said Lasvarg as he ate the bird raw, since he had no flame to cook it.

"And I shall call you Lord Sparks," said the boy now called Gull. "For I saw sparks when you were trying to summon your dragon flames."

Lasvarg, who would henceforth be known by the name Lord Sparks, growled, thinking the boy was mocking him with this name, and spat the seagull bones into the sea.

"I shall not stay here with you, insolent boy," he grumbled. "It is a barren and hostile place. Already hounds gather at the foot of that obelisk. Hounds and dragons do not mix well."

Gull heard a noise in the distance and jumped up onto a rock for a better view. "And there is a ship docked at the jetty, bristling with so many spears it is like a porcupine on the waves."

"Spears," said Lord Sparks, rubbing his side. "I do not like spears."

And with that, the dragon spread his mighty wings, filling the membranes like sails, and rose up over the boy.

"I will fly far from here where men with spears and boys with jibes will not test my patience," he declared.

For some reason the notion of the dragon leaving filled the boy with dread, even though Lord Sparks was no friend to him so far as he knew—not that he seemed to know much of anything. Perhaps it was the bristling hounds watching him or else the bristling spears in the ship that disconcerted him so. Either way, Gull, his head a fog of confused thoughts, felt suddenly desperate to leave this inhospitable place.

"Take me with you, sir dragon," he begged. "I meant no offense, and I can be useful."

The dragon looked down sharply at this slightly built youth.

"And how might a scrawny boy be useful to a mighty dragon?"

This indeed was a question.

To which Gull might have had a long list of answers once upon a time, but now he could for the life of him think of only one.

"I can cook birds," he said, though he was not sure if even this much was true.

The dragon hovered in place considering this, still tasting the bitter gull meat between his teeth.

"Very well, boy," he said finally, reaching down to grab Gull by the shoulders with powerful claws. "You may cook birds for me, but no more jibes or you will find yourself in the pot."

With the dragon's talons clamped on his shoulders, the boy was in no position to argue, and before he could agree to *No more jibes*, Lord Sparks flew them away from the Isle of Salt with such fierce velocity that the words were stuffed back down into his lungs.

CHAPTER SEVEN

The Vagabond Years

THE BOY GULL LEARNED TO ROAST A BIRD, FOR IT WAS NO GREAT thing to hang a spit over a fire, but that was the extent of his invention, and as he grew older he found himself less concerned with ideas and more interested in satisfying his own day-to-day needs and those of his master, the irascible Lord Sparks. Gull grew into a man who preferred to solve problems with his fists, and it was not long before the pair had made a reputation for themselves as useful laborers who would take on any job for coin.

Lord Sparks's distrust of humans grew ever more entrenched, and he would eat nothing but food prepared by Gull for fear of it being poisoned. He seemed to have a constant pain in his gut and could only imagine it had got there through poisoning in his younger days. In this the dragon was correct, as the poisoned spearhead that had penetrated his hide on the Isle of Salt was putrefying his insides and slowly working its way to his heart.

Over the years Gull and Lord Sparks grew grudgingly inseparable for reasons they could not quite remember, and both assumed it had always been this way. They fought in a dozen wars across the continent, hiring themselves out to kings and emperors, and with every punch thrown, another layer of scar tissue grew over Gull's mind so that in time there was not even a trace left of the boy he had once been.

The pair communicated as little as possible and often passed several weeks in each other's company without speaking a word. Gull prepared the food and Lord Sparks ate it. The only indication that there was any form of friendship between the two was that perhaps three midwinter nights a year Lord Sparks would allow Gull to sleep underneath his wing, and only then because if the man were to freeze, there would be no cooked breakfast the following morning.

By this time, nearly half a century had passed and Gull was on his last legs so far as his career as any kind of knight, soldier, or fairground roustabout was concerned. His eyes were rheumed, his joints cracked like dry twigs, and the plates of his armor were barely more than patches of rust daubed with paint. Lord Sparks too was much reduced, though he should not have been, for dragons can live a thousand years, but not if their insides are corrupted by dark magic poison.

They traveled the land searching for casual labor, but people either were fearful of Lord Sparks's scowling snout or had little use for a dragon without fire, and so the unlikely pair were forced by circumstance to take on increasingly hazardous labor, such as digging in a mountainside sulfur mine, net-hoisting in the stormy waters of the Northern Sea, and finally nest-scraping on the Sun Tower of Belenos.

"Belenos is a new one," Lord Sparks muttered when he first saw the glittering shard. "The tower is older than the god it's named for. A relic from another kingdom I'd wager."

Nest-scraping was just as ignoble as it sounded. The scraper's job was to scale the copper-plated tower and dislodge both the osprey nests and any mess the birds had left behind so that the tower might remain a gleaming tribute to the sun god Belenos. There were three main difficulties with being a nest-scraper. It was high-altitude work, the winds were unpredictable, and the tower's shape attracted lightning. None of these factors should have been any trouble to a dragon, but Lord Sparks's poison-infused organs caused him daily pain and made each flight more of an effort than it should have been.

Gull, for his part, had the arduous job of hoisting himself aloft on a pulley system and cleaning any smears he could reach. And more than once, as he scrubbed at a particularly ingrained smear of bird dropping, Gull thought to himself, *This tower seems familiar somehow, as though I have been here long ago.*

On the pair's final day as nest-scrapers, more than half a century after they'd left the Isle of Salt, Lord Sparks flapped laboriously to the tip of the copper tower and began his usual routine of scaring off the birds before dislodging their nests with the tip of a claw. Gull scrubbed the lower section, calling encouragement through a leather cone and promising to cook the dragon's favorite fowl stew for supper. But the idea of a tasty supper would not be enough to spur the dragon on today, for the

spearhead in his chest was now pressing against the very membrane of his heart, while the poison corrupted even the dragon's mind. The top of the tower seemed very far away to Lord Sparks, but he would not give in and with one last mighty lunge grasped the spire.

It was at this precise moment that the spearhead pierced the membrane of Lord Sparks's heart, and this at last proved too much. The dragon clutched his chest, which suddenly seemed too small to accommodate the pounding organ within. The tremendous pain, greater than any the dragon could ever remember, was surely fatal, for how could there be life after such agony? The dragon wrapped his wings around the tower, hooking them together as dragons do when sleeping in high aeries, and so did not fall when his once mighty heart beat its last.

However, this is not the end of Lasvarg's story, for as the dragon clung to the Sun Tower, a bolt of lightning struck the spire and was conducted through the copper and into the dragon himself, dislodging him just as easily as he had dislodged osprey nests for so many years. The dragon plummeted senseless to earth, bashing into the tower's copper walls several times on his descent.

Gull watched these events from below, appalled at the dragon's trials. Though they had never been friends, the two relied completely on each other, and Gull had never imagined that the dragon would be first to die. Who would provide for him now?

But Gull was wrong—the lightning bolt had not shocked the life from the dragon but rather shocked the life back *into* him, and as he tumbled toward the stone plinth at the foot of the tower, the memories of his previous life returned. As he had in effect died, Delbayne's curse was immediately lifted.

For his part, the old man Gull was gripped by terror as he saw the spotted hand with which he now shielded his eyes soften to that of a mere boy, and he cried, "Witchcraft!"

Again Gull was mistaken. It was not witchcraft but sorcery, and as the curse was lifted, the decades rolled back and Gull became Lir once more. A great dark magic

94

rose from his body in a
cloud of smoke and the man
who was a boy once more collapsed to the
stone flags. Before Lir fell unconscious he heard two mighty
cracks. The first was the sound of the lightning finally regis-
tering in his ears, and the second was Lasvarg's bulk smashing
through two layers of granite beside him.

Lasvarg, he thought. *I remember.*

· · · · · · · · · ·

Lasvarg and Lir lay on the flagstones for some time as their own
stories flowed through them. The curse had been lifted by the dragon's
momentary death. In the place of an over-the-hill workhorse was a
noble dragon, and in the stead of an aged bruiser there lay a young
scientist with barely enough years to grow scruff on his cheeks.

It was the boy who moved first: he sat up and saw that where
Lasvarg's fall had knocked off the tower's copper plating, there was
pale rock below.

It is the Wolfhound's Tooth, he realized. *I am home.*

He shook off his battered armor and tried to revive his friend with
a gentle shaking.

"Sir dragon," he said. "Lasvarg. It is I, Lir."

The dragon made an
attempt at a smile, but it was
plain to the prince that even though the
dragon had returned from the dead, it would
not be for long. Lasvarg was dying. The fall had done him in.

Lasvarg coughed and said weakly, "Lir, my friend, I shall die on the
Isle of Salt with my friends around me. Take me home."

• • • • • • • • •

It was a long and strange journey through a country so utterly changed in only half a century. Lir asked questions of passersby and found that his beloved city of Lagin had been overrun by raiders no fewer than three times, and the days of stability that Lir had known during his father's reign were little more than a cherished memory among a population who had been cruelly taxed for years to pay for the Sun Tower's copper cladding. Lir's heart ached for the home of his youth, and he vowed to return as soon as he was able. But for now his thoughts were mostly of Cethlenn and how he was terrified he would arrive too late to save her.

Perhaps the amber did not hold, he thought.

Lir hired a wagon and passed through the city, which had nothing more left from the Wulfson days other than a wolfhound statue with

features worn down by southerly winds that were as biting as ever. And from there the boy and the dragon traveled to the docks, which had silted just enough to choke off trade, leaving only enough draft for small fishing boats and a ferry to the archipelago. Lir glanced up from the harbor to the spot on the hill where the royal palace once loomed and saw there was nothing left but the ruin of a burnt-out castle and stories of a mad queen whose kingdom had been overrun by bandits.

Lir draped the dragon carefully in a waxed cloth and helped him board a trawler bound for the deep fishing grounds. The captain needed persuading with the last of their wages to dock at the Isle of Salt, for it had become overrun with mad dogs and there were rumors of altercations between the hounds and the occasional troupe of treasure hunters seeking the fabled dragon's treasure.

When they arrived at the Isle of Salt's jetty, which was now barely more than a gathering of spindly sticks, the shaggy pack of wolfhounds sniffed at the ankles of the two visitors as they disembarked, but made no move to attack. In fact, Lir and Lasvarg found themselves with a growling honor guard all the way to the amber monolith, which was crusted with shellfish, seaweed, and a white curtain of dried salt.

Lir led Lasvarg to lie down on a flat stone; it was clear from the dragon's labored breath that he was near the end.

"It is too late," wheezed Lasvarg. "I am done."

"You must try," said Lir gently.

Lasvarg nodded. He had to try. The dragon rolled himself on all fours and gnashed his jaws, hoping he could summon sparks one last time. On the second try they came, a soft haze like fireflies in the blackness of his throat.

For a moment, the dragon was his old mighty self, and he felt the amber surge from his gorge as his instinct to breathe flame grew irresistible.

Lir could only stand back and watch this rare sight, the mythical dragon's breath. And while the scientist in him knew it was a natural chemical phenomenon, at that moment it seemed magical.

The flame was beautiful and complex, with many colors floating inside the blast like a bolt of bright fabric. Such a flame could never be resisted, and the second it licked the obelisk, the amber began slowly to melt, sloughing away in collapsing globs.

"Very well," rasped Lasvarg, sinking back, his eyes growing dim. "It is done. I am sorry, my friend, for your father. Remember me only for my labors on this day."

Lir's tears dripped on the dragon's broad snout. "I too am sorry. Your likes shall not be seen again."

"My time is past, it is true," said Lasvarg. "But now is the time of humankind and machines. *Your* time, boy."

The dragon died as all things do, with a last breath, and Lir watched as the ancient magical hide instantly fossilized, leaving a rough statue of Lasvarg on the rock shelf behind him.

Lir knew he would mourn the dragon for the rest of his life, but for now he turned his attention to Cethlenn.

The melting amber spread in a pool that smelled of clover honey and set the wolfhounds howling and gamboling in preparation for the rebirth of their queen. The outer layers fell away to reveal the deep ochre of the amber itself and inside the figure of Cethlenn, alive or preserved Lir could not yet tell.

Finally the inner casing split with a thunderclap, and the entire front section dropped forward like a makeshift staircase.

The wolfhounds surged forward, blanketing their queen, and try as Lir might, he could not clear a path to her. For every dog he dragged away, a dozen took its place.

"Leave her," he cried, sinking to his knees. "Leave her be."

The young prince felt overwhelmed, friendless and defeated and certain that now he would lose even Cethlenn's body to a frenzied pack of wolfhounds.

But then the hounds fell silent, and Lir looked up to see them, heads bowed, muzzles low to the ground, as Cethlenn stepped down from the fractured obelisk with sparks playing in her hair.

She smiled at Lir and asked, "Have you returned to ask me again?"

Lir felt his heart soar for the first time in many years, and he answered joyfully.

"Yes, my queen. I have returned to ask you again. Our kingdom has failed and our people starve. You must return to bring light and hope."

Cethlenn sat on the rock beside Lir, resting her back gently against what had been Lasvarg's body.

"I will think on it, Prince Lir, but first I have a request to make of you."

"Anything," said Lir. "Anything that a man may do, I shall do."

Cethlenn smiled again. "It has been such a long time since we sat on these same rocks and shared a meal, so I wonder if you might cook me a fish."

Lir laughed at this. He was happy to prepare honey fish for them
both, and as they talked, laughed, and cried, the heat trapped inside
the dragon's mighty chest kept them warm through the night.